DISNEY

MICKEY MOUSE CLUBHOUSE

Mickey's Mystery List

Read along as Mickey Mouse follows some strange clues on a special shopping list. You will know it is time to turn the page when you hear this sound.... Ready? Let's begin!

publications international, ltd.

One morning, Minnie Mouse opens up her window and looks out at the sunny sky.

"What a beautiful day to go shopping," says Minnie. "Especially surprise-party shopping."

Minnie looks at her special shopping list. Minnie, Goofy, Donald, and Daisy have written a list of things they need for a surprise party. To make sure the party stays a secret, they've written rhyming riddles for all the items they need!

"This will be the most wonderful party ever!" says Minnie. She writes "Clubhouse Surprise Shopping List" at the top of the page.

As Minnie walks toward town, a gust of wind blows the list out of her hand. Minnie turns quickly to catch it, but it flies up in the air and behind some trees.

Minnie looks all over for the list but cannot find it anywhere!

"Oh, my!" says Minnie. "Without the list, the surprise party will be ruined!"

Minnie sadly returns to the Clubhouse and tells the rest of the gang what happened. Everyone agrees to help Minnie find the list.

Meanwhile, Mickey is playing fetch with Pluto.

"Go fetch, boy!" calls Mickey as he throws a stick. Pluto chases after the stick, but when he returns, he's carrying a piece of paper instead.

"What's that, Pluto?" asks Mickey. Mickey looks at the paper and sees the words "Clubhouse Surprise Shopping List" written on the top.

"Oh boy!" says Mickey. "Somebody at the Clubhouse is preparing a special surprise!"

Then Mickey has a great idea for a surprise of his own! "I'll collect all of the items on the list and bring them to the Clubhouse! I'll surprise the surprisers!"

Mickey sees that all the items on the list are written as rhyming riddles. The first riddle is:

"Two words that Mickey likes to say
Are a 'tasty snack' for a special day!"

Mickey thinks really hard. "Hot dog, that's a tough one," he says. "Wait a minute — that's it! Hot dogs are a tasty snack!"

Mickey and Pluto go to the grocery store and get hot dogs, buns, and mustard. Mickey asks Pluto to take the hot dogs back to the Clubhouse while he continues shopping with the list.

Mickey looks at the next riddle on the list:
"Our party we will decorate
With plants that look and smell just great."

Mickey scratches his head. "Hmm, I bet Daisy would know the answer to this one," he says. "Hey! A daisy is a type of plant that looks and smells great! I bet we need flowers!"

Mickey goes to the flower store and collects several beautiful bouquets.

"I'll be sure to get some daisies for Daisy!" he says.

the Flower Spot

Back at the Clubhouse, Minnie and all her friends set out to find the missing list.

Daisy peeks under a blueberry bush. "No, not there," says Daisy.

Donald looks up a tree. "Phooey!" says Donald. "I don't see it!"

Goofy even goes to look in a cornfield. "Gawrsh! This is very corn-fusing!"

Minnie is worried they won't ever find the list.

While his friends look for the list, Mickey looks at the next riddle:
"*For the next step, we've all agreed,*
We'll get our friend a gift to read."
Mickey thinks for a while, then snaps his fingers! "Something to read? Why, that's a book!"

Mickey goes into the bookstore and sees a book next to a sign that says "reserved."

"This must be the one," says Mickey. He looks at the book's title. "Hmm, *Mousekedoer Mechanics*. I'm sure that'll come in real handy!"

"This is shaping up to be a great surprise," says Mickey as he looks at the next clue:

> *"Our guest is certain to enjoy*
> *This sporty, speedy, two-wheeled toy."*

"I wonder what it could be," says Mickey. Mickey thinks of toys that are sporty and have two wheels. "Maybe it's a bike!"

Mickey goes to the bicycle store and sees a bike with a bow on it. "Hot dog! This must be it!" he says.

Mickey looks at the next item on the list:

"For this surprise, please don't forget
A doggy treat for our pal's pet!"

"This one's easy," says Mickey. Thanks to Pluto, Mickey knows that all dogs love to chew bones. Mickey heads to the pet store and picks out the biggest bone he can find.

"Oh, boy," says Mickey. "I'm almost at the end of the list! Where to next?"

Mickey reads the next clue:

"*For our party, we all know that*
  Each guest will need a party ____."

"Gee!" says Mickey. "The last word is missing." Mickey guesses that the last word must rhyme with the word "that."

"I'd better put my thinking hat on," says Mickey. "Hot dog! That's it! Party guests need party hats, and 'hat' rhymes with 'that!'"

Mickey goes to the hat store and gets some great hats for the party. Then he gathers up all the goodies and rushes back to the Clubhouse.

Just as Mickey arrives at the Clubhouse, he notices one more riddle on the back of the list:

"*Our last surprise we'll bake with care:*
A sweet dessert for friends to share."

Mickey is sad that he did not get all the items, but when he walks into the Clubhouse he sees that his friends are sad too.

Mickey asks Minnie what's the matter, and she explains about the lost list.

"Well, the good news is I found your list, and collected most of the items on it!" says Mickey. "The bad news is I didn't get the very last thing."

When Mickey's friends discover that he's collected all the items on the list, they laugh and shout for joy.

"Oh, Mickey!" says Minnie. "That surprise list was a list we made for you! We wanted to throw you a surprise birthday party!"